The Ghost of Uncle Arvie

Sharon Creech is an American who lived in England for nineteen years. She now lives in New Jersey, USA, where her husband is headmaster of a boarding school.

Sharon is well known for her fiction for older children. *Walk Two Moons* was shortlisted for the 1995 Smarties Book Prize and won the 1995 Newbery Medal, awarded to 'the most distinguished contribution to American literature for children published in 1994'. It was also the winner of the 1995 Children's Book Award and the WH Smith Mind-Boggling Books Award 1996. Her novel *Ruby Holler* won the 2002 Carnegie Medal.

Shock Shop is a superb collection of short, illustrated, scary books for younger readers by some of today's most acclaimed writers for children.

Other titles in Shock Shop:

SHOCK SHOP

The Ghost of Uncle Arvie

Sharon Creech

Illustrated by Simon Cooper

MACMILLAN CHILDREN'S BOOKS

First published 1996 by Macmillan Children's Books

This edition published 2004 by Macmillan Children's Books
a division of Macmillan Publishers Limited
20 New Wharf Road, London N1 9RR
Basingstoke and Oxford
www.panmacmillan.com

Associated companies throughout the world

ISBN 0 330 34212 6

1 3 5 7 9 8 6 4 2

A CIP catalogue record for this book is available from
the British Library.

Typeset by Intype Libra Ltd
Printed and bound in Great Britain by Mackays of Chatham plc, Kent

For the TASIS Lower School's Young Authors

CONTENTS

CHAPTER ONE
With the Wind

Another ghost arrived last week.

Once or twice a year, a ghost visits me – a different ghost each time. The ghosts come with the wind at night. It isn't an ordinary wind, but a bare whisper of wind which tickles the curtains. No one sees or hears this wind except me and my dog Bo.

I am your basic, ordinary, nine year-old boy, and usually I live a basic, ordinary life. I go to school, I tend to my dog Bo, I eat, I sleep. My name is Danny. Sometimes, though, my life is not so ordinary. This is because of the ghosts.

The first ghost came when I was five years old. It was my great gran, but I didn't know she was a ghost. She seemed real enough to me. When I mentioned Great Gran's visit to my mother, she said, "Danny, Great Gran is in heaven."

"Not last night she wasn't," I said.

"Danny, Great Gran is dead. She's in heaven."

1

The next year, my old cat Choo flew in my bedroom window. When I held his puckered old face up to my mother, she pressed her hand against my forehead. "Oh, Danny," she said. "Not feeling well? Choo's been dead for six months."

There have been other ghosts since: an old man who used to live next door, a woman who said she had lived two hundred years ago, and a policeman. I asked the policeman ghost, "Why do ghosts visit me? Why don't they visit anyone else I know?"

The policeman said he couldn't say for sure.

"Why did *you* come to visit me?" I asked.

"I was just out riding on the wind, and this is where it brought me."

Imagine! To ride on the wind and whiz into people's windows like that!

Last Friday, as I climbed into bed, I heard one of the whispering winds. When my mother looked in to say goodnight, I asked her if a storm was coming.

"Storm? No, I don't think so. Look how calm it is. Not even a breeze out there."

So I knew that this was a ghost wind. Soon,

it would be followed by a faint whistle, and then the wind would swirl and roll and twist in through the room trailing a cloud of blue smoke. Out of that blue smoke would step a ghost. That's how it happens.

The ghosts had never hurt me, but still I was afraid. What if it was a wicked, horrible ghost? But I was also interested. I wanted to know who it would be. Maybe it would be the one ghost I wanted, the one ghost I prayed for.

My dog Bo whimpered in his sleep. Did he sense what was coming? The wind whistled, and the curtains curled in the air. Bo's yellow fur stood on end.

I had an odd, quivery feeling.

I've tried to tell my friends and teachers about these ghosts, but they just laugh. "What an imagination!" my teachers say. One boy at school, Billy Baker, punched me in the chest. "You don't see no ghosts, you stupid liar," he said.

The wind blew harder, reeling and rolling through the window, twisting the curtains high into the air. Bo crawled up beside me and covered his ears with his paws.

3

"Get ready, Bo. Here comes the ghost."

Whish! blew the wind. *Whew!* The curtains flew this way and that, knocking a book off my desk. *Wisk!* My socks lifted off the floor and danced in the air.

Bo scooted around in a circle, trying to get his head under the covers.

Whish! Wisk! The curtains flipped into the air and sank down again, wrapping their ends around the chair. Suddenly, the wind calmed. In came a quiet stream of air and a wisp of blue smoke which swirled and floated across the room.

"Here it comes, Bo. We're about to have a visitor."

The blue smoke twisted and twirled, floating down to the floor and forming itself into a pair of feet, covered in green boots.

"It's here, Bo."

The smoke formed two sturdy legs in blue trousers. Next appeared a purple sweater across a big chest and arms. The smoke wiggled and wobbled and formed into a head topped by a red cowboy hat.

The ghost had arrived.

CHAPTER TWO
The Ghost

I recognized him immediately. "Uncle Arvie?" I said. "It's you, isn't it?"

"Riggle!" said the ghost, brushing himself off.

It was Uncle Arvie all right. That's just the way Uncle Arvie talks – or *used* to talk, when he was alive. You could hardly understand a word he said.

Bo poked his nose out from under the blanket, sniffed the air, and barked. I lifted the blanket and removed Bo's paws from his eyes. Bo tilted his head from side to side, staring at Uncle Arvie.

"Can you see him?" I asked Bo. "It's Uncle Arvie."

"Yip," Bo squeaked.

"Elephant?" Uncle Arvie said.

"No, it's my dog."

"Elephant!" Uncle Arvie insisted.

This was not going to be an easy ghost to have around.

When I was little, Uncle Arvie spoke just like everyone else, saying normal words at the normal time. You could understand him. But one day – when Uncle Arvie was still alive – he woke up speaking this way.

Uncle Arvie had had a stroke and words were twisted in his brain. He knew what he *wanted* to say, but the words that came out of his mouth were not the words he chose. Sometimes they were not even words at all – or at least not words that anyone could understand – like *riggle* and *pailandplop*.

"You're supposed to be in heaven now," I said.

"Railroad, yin."

"Heaven – up there."

Uncle Arvie waved his arms as if he were flying. "Railroad!"

He strolled around my room, looking at things. He picked up the book that had fallen on the floor. "Pasta," he said. "Wig pasta." Next, he examined the pictures on my bookshelf, picking up one of me and my mother. "Macaroni and Dinosaur!" he said.

"It's my mother and me – *Danny*," I said.

"Macaroni and Dinosaur! Macaroni and Dinosaur!"

Why couldn't I get a normal ghost? What was I going to do with this ghost?

Uncle Arvie examined a photograph of my father. He kissed the picture. "Dinosaur's pepperoni," he said. Uncle Arvie pointed towards the door. "Pepperoni?"

"My father isn't here."

"Nod pepperoni?"

"He's gone. He . . ."

Uncle Arvie tilted his head just like Bo, waiting for me to finish.

"He's in heaven," I said.

"Nod!" Uncle Arvie put his hands over his mouth. "Nod railroad? Nod pepperoni railroad? Nod, nod." He was very upset. My father and Uncle Arvie were brothers.

"I was hoping maybe you'd seen him there – in heaven."

"Nod, nod," Uncle Arvie cried. "Nod, nod pepperoni."

I gave him a tissue. "It was last year," I said. "Right after you. He was very sick."

Uncle Arvie blew his nose.

"We miss him," I said.

Uncle Arvie held the picture to his chest.

"We miss you, too," I said.

Uncle Arvie put the picture back on the book-shelf and lifted another photograph. It was one of Uncle Arvie and his wife Julia.

"Oh, Heartfoot," he said. "Oh, oh, Heartfoot." He hugged the picture and kissed it.

"*She's* not in heaven," I was glad to report. "Julia's fine!"

"Oh, Heartfoot." He put the picture back and turned suddenly. "Please," he begged. "Three please."

"What?"

Uncle Arvie held up four fingers, looked at them, and then pushed one back down. Three fingers wiggled.

"Three what?" I asked. It looked as if Uncle Arvie wanted three things, but I had no idea what he might want. "Food?"

"Nod."

"Money?"

"Nod, nod."

"Clothes?"

"Nod, nod, nod." He waggled his fingers in my face.

"Nail clippers?"

"Nod!"

I was getting a little annoyed. "Maybe we should sleep now," I said. I hoped that in the morning, I'd be able to understand him better. Or maybe he'd be gone. I really would have preferred a ghost who spoke normally.

Uncle Arvie glanced pitifully at his three fingers.

"Maybe I'll understand in the morning," I said. "Maybe we should get some sleep—"

"Stamp," Uncle Arvie said. He lay down on top of my desk, with his long legs sticking straight out in the air over the edge, as if they were held up by something invisible. Soon he was snoring. Bo wriggled out from beneath the blanket, sniffed the air, and whimpered.

"Well, Bo, we have a new ghost. Try to be brave." I patted Bo's head until he closed his eyes.

There was no more wind. All was quiet except for the snoring of Uncle Arvie and of Bo. The curtains hung straight against the window, and outside I could see the black sky and the bright stars.

I found a star and on it I wished: "It would be nice to have another ghost. I wish for . . ." I thought about what Uncle Arvie had called my father. "I wish for . . . for my *pepperoni*."

Uncle Arvie was thrashing this way and that in his sleep. He was still wearing his boots, clothes, and red hat. I was surprised that ghosts slept with their clothes on. I had thought that maybe they had special white robes to sleep in.

I hoped that tomorrow I could figure out what Uncle Arvie meant by "three pleases". I hoped he wouldn't expect me to steal anything for him. And why did he need me to help him anyway? I thought ghosts could do whatever they wanted.

I wondered if I should tell my mother that Uncle Arvie's ghost was visiting. No. She would say that Uncle Arvie was in heaven. There was no such thing as a ghost.

CHAPTER THREE

The First Please

I was so scared. I was running down a railroad track, faster and faster, and there was a terrible noise behind me. I turned, expecting to see a train barrelling down on me, but it wasn't a train. It was a gigantic Tyrannosaurus Rex wearing a wig made of spaghetti. Someone was shouting, "Dinosaur! Dinosaur!"

I sat straight up in bed. What a nightmare. What a relief to be safe—

"Dinosaur! Dinosaur!"

Floating up near the ceiling was Uncle Arvie, calling me. Bo quivered underneath the blanket.

"Dinosaur!"

"I'm awake," I said.

"Good carpet!"

I looked down at the old, soiled carpet on my floor. It was not a good carpet at all.

Uncle Arvie stretched his arms wide and breathed deeply. "Good carpet, Dinosaur!"

"Good *morning*?" I guessed.

"Good carpet!"

Bo thumped his tail and the blanket flopped up and down. There was a knock at my door. "Danny? You awake?"

My heart wobbled. Would my mother be able to see Uncle Arvie? What would she say? Should I warn her?

"You're up early for a Saturday, aren't you?" she said, opening the door. Bo bounded out of the bed and leaped up against her, wagging his tail and barking. "Easy, Bo, easy," my mother said. "Looks like he's ready for a walk, Danny. Guess you'll have to get up."

Uncle Arvie was standing behind my mother, smiling at her.

"Macaroni," Uncle Arvie said. "Feather macaroni."

"Did you hear that?" I asked her.

"Hear what?"

"Do you see anything over there?"

"Sure do."

"You *do*? You actually, really and truly *do*?" I said.

"Yes. I see books on the floor, socks in a heap. It's kind of a mess, isn't it?"

She didn't see Uncle Arvie. And yet, to me, Uncle Arvie was as clear as could be. The only difference between Uncle Arvie and my mother was that Uncle Arvie looked a bit blurry around the edges.

The edges of Uncle Arvie's red cowboy hat wobbled, as if the hat were alive. His purple sweater was slightly shimmery, almost as if it were breathing. The same was true of his trousers and boots – they shimmered at the sides, growing darker, then dimmer.

My mother sniffed the air. "What's that smell?"

Maybe she could *smell* the ghost, I thought.

She picked up my socks. "These should go in the wash," she said. "And there's some other smell – what is it?" She glanced around the room. "It reminds me of . . . of someone. I can't think who it is."

Uncle Arvie was waving his arms all around. "Pin!" Uncle Arvie said. "Pin!"

My mother dropped the socks on to my bed. "Bring these down with your other dirty clothes," she said as she left. "I'll feed Bo, but you'd better be ready to walk him pretty soon."

"I don't understand it," I said to Uncle Arvie. "She can't see you or hear you, and yet I can see and hear you as clear as anything."

Uncle Arvie zoomed up to the ceiling, flipped twice and landed on my bed. "Three please? Three please?"

I had forgotten about that, and now that I was reminded, I was a little worried. "Let's take Bo out, and you can explain as we walk," I suggested.

"Pin mailer," Uncle Arvie said, flapping his arms. "Pin mailer, mailer, mailer!" He flapped his arms, lifted into the air and sailed smoothly through the window.

Bo barked and jumped against the window ledge. His long tail whacked my legs. "No, Bo," I said, "you can't go through the window."

Uncle Arvie floated across the road, circled a tree, and skimmed lightly to the ground. It was probably fortunate that Uncle Arvie was wearing his green boots, because he had landed in a puddle. He stood there grinning up at us.

Bo bounded down the stairs, out of the door, and stopped at the kerb, wagging his tail. I led him across the street, and he leaped towards Uncle Arvie, barking and wiggling his back end.

"One please?" Uncle Arvie said.

"I'll try," I said. "What is it?"

"Fraggle pin Heartfoot a wig pasta, and—"

"Wait a minute!" I said. "I didn't exactly get that. Could you repeat it?"

Uncle Arvie put his hands to his eyes and formed two circles, as if he were looking through binoculars. "Fraggle pin Heartfoot—"

"Heartfoot – that's your wife, right? Julia? You want me to see Aunt Julia – show her something?"

"Yin!"

"What do you want me to show her?"

"Wig pasta," Uncle Arvie said.

This sounded familiar. Uncle Arvie had said "wig pasta" last night. When did he say it? What was he looking at? "My socks?" I said.

"Nod, nod."

I thought again. "The book?"

"Wig pasta! Wig pasta!" Uncle Arvie said. "Yin."

"You want me to show Aunt Julia my book?"

17

"Nod Dinosaur wig pasta. *Pin* wig pasta," Uncle Arvie said.

"You want me to show her *your* book?"

"Yin! Pin wig pasta!"

"Well, OK. Is the book at your house?"

"Yin!"

That sounded easy enough, I thought. I'd take Uncle Arvie to see Aunt Julia, and we'd find the book and show it to her. I could not imagine why this was so important to Uncle Arvie. Was there something special about the book? Would Aunt Julia be able to see her husband?

CHAPTER FOUR
Deester in the Wig Pasta

On the way to Aunt Julia's, I asked Uncle Arvie why he didn't go to his house last night to see her. He spread out his arms and turned around and around and tripped and fell to the ground. "Pailandplop."

"You couldn't steer?"

"Yin. Pailandplop."

"Will she be able to see you?" I asked.

"Nod." Uncle Arvie sniffed. "Nod fraggle."

"Why not?"

Uncle Arvie shrugged. He didn't know.

"Couldn't *you* show her the wig pasta – the book, I mean?"

"Nod." Uncle Arvie shook all over. "Heart-foot twiggle a twiggle!" He trembled and looked afraid. He opened his mouth and screamed.

Bo barked and hid behind me. "Oh, it would frighten her," I said.

"Yin, twiggle, twiggle," Uncle Arvie agreed.

When we arrived at Aunt Julia's house, Uncle

Arvie clapped his hands. "Pin box," he said. "Pin and Heartfoot box."

"Danny?" Aunt Julia said, opening the door. "What a lovely surprise."

Uncle Arvie put his hands to his chest. "Oh, Heartfoot! Good carpet, Heartfoot!"

But she could not see him and she did not hear him. She leaned down and kissed me and patted Bo. "Come on in," she said. "I have company already. We were just having tea."

Uncle Arvie smiled at everything he saw. He touched the walls and the furniture. He took a deep breath, as if he wanted to breathe in everything.

"Come on into the kitchen," Aunt Julia said. "I want you to meet my company."

In the kitchen was a tall, skinny man with greasy black hair. When he smiled, I saw two silver teeth.

"Here," Aunt Julia said. "This is Colin."

"Nod!" Uncle Arvie said. "Nod pin box! Nod beany booger." Uncle Arvie did not like the look of Colin. He apparently did not like another man being in his house.

"What are you looking at, Danny? Is something wrong?" Aunt Julia said. "And what on earth is wrong with Bo?"

Bo was quivering beside me as Uncle Arvie shouted, "Nod beany booger a pin box!" I couldn't believe that Aunt Julia could not see or hear Uncle Arvie. He was flailing all around, shouting and waving his arms.

"Danny? What *are* you staring at?" she repeated.

"Oh nothing – sorry," I said.

Aunt Julia sniffed the air. "What's that smell? It reminds me of . . ." She stopped and shook her head. "No, it's silly of me."

She offered me some biscuits. Colin sat down and smiled his silvery smile at me and at Aunt Julia. I did not like the look of him either.

She brought a vase of white freesias to the table. "Look what Colin brought me. Wasn't that sweet? Don't they smell lovely?"

"Nod!" Uncle Arvie shouted. "Nod!" Uncle Arvie pushed the vase off the table. It fell with a loud crash to the floor and broke into pieces. Bo barked.

"Oh!" Aunt Julia said. "How on earth . . . ? What happened? My goodness!"

Colin stared at the broken vase.

"Danny, why don't you and Colin go on into the other room while I clean up this mess? Oh goodness, I can't imagine how this happened."

I went straight to the bookcase and looked at the titles. Which one did Uncle Arvie want me to show Aunt Julia?

Colin stood beside me. "Do you like books?" he asked.

"I guess."

"I don't, not much," Colin said. "Gives me a headache to read a book."

"Beany booger," Uncle Arvie said. "Beany bud booger."

Uncle Arvie examined the shelf. He looked and looked, at row after row of books. At last he said, "Wig pasta!" and just as he reached for a book, Colin reached up, and took that same book from the shelf. "Nod!" Uncle Arvie said. "Nod pin wig pasta beany booger."

Colin leafed through the pages. "Now this book would definitely give me a headache," Colin said. "The print is too small."

"May I see it?" I asked.

"Sure, just a minute. Wait, what's this?" Colin had found something in the book. It looked like a letter.

Aunt Julia appeared, carrying a tray of sandwiches and biscuits. "Here we are," she said. "Now we can have a proper tea."

Uncle Arvie was going crazy. "Pin wig pasta a deester! Pin deester!"

I turned to help Aunt Julia with the tray, and when I looked back at Colin, I saw an astonishing thing. Colin took the letter from the book and put it in his pocket. Bo must have seen this too, because he growled at Colin.

Uncle Arvie clutched his chest. "Pin deester a Heartfoot!" He pulled at Colin's jacket, trying to get the letter.

"Hey," Colin said, brushing at his jacket. "Is there something on me?"

Uncle Arvie pinched Colin's arm.

"Hey!" Colin said. "A wasp!" He took off his jacket and stomped on it.

"Why, Colin dear, whatever is the matter? A wasp? Are you OK?" She examined Colin's arm.

Bo dragged the jacket into the kitchen.

"Beany booger!" Uncle Arvie said, pinching Colin's other arm.

"Hey!" Colin wailed. "Another one?" He slapped at his arm.

"Oh goodness, goodness," Aunt Julia said.

In the kitchen Bo was scratching at Colin's jacket. "Here, I'll get it," I said. On the envelope was written, "Pin Heartfoot." I stuffed the letter in my own pocket and took Colin's jacket back to him.

Uncle Arvie must have pinched Colin again, because Colin was saying, "Hey! Hey!" Colin swung at the air and slapped at his neck. "I'm going!" Colin said.

"Oh goodness," Aunt Julia said.

I handed Colin his jacket and he rushed out of the door.

"Beany booger," Uncle Arvie said.

"Aunt Julia," I said. "I was looking at one of your books and I found something. I think it's for you." I gave her the letter.

"Oh!" She clasped her hands to her mouth and kissed the envelope. "It's from Arvie!" She tore open the envelope and read the note inside. "Look," she said, pointing to the date on it. "It was written the day before Arvie died." A tear ran down her cheek. "Listen, it's a poem." She read:

> "Heartfoot a lalley
> Heartfoot a sweel
> Pin Heartfoot pin Heartfoot
> Pin Heartfoot a teel."

"Oh, how lovely, how sweet," she said.

Uncle Arvie was staring at her. He looked both sad and happy at the same time.

"What does it mean?" I asked.

"Well," she said. "I'm not entirely sure. *Heartfoot* – that's me, Julia. That's what he called me after his stroke. And *pin* – that usually meant *me* or *my*. But I don't know what *lalley* or *sweel* or *teel* mean. It's still lovely, though. I'm sure it's a love poem."

Bo put his head on her foot and slobbered.

"I bet this was for my birthday," she said. "I see he didn't forget it after all."

She read the poem again and again. Once she looked up and sniffed the air. "That smell," she said. "Doesn't it smell like – like Arvie?"

Uncle Arvie leaned down and kissed her

cheek. She couldn't see him, but she must have felt something, because she put her hand to her cheek.

"I'm feeling a little peculiar," she said. "I think I'll lie down. But thank you for finding this. I might never ever have discovered it."

I thought Uncle Arvie might stay with Aunt Julia, but he followed me and Bo out of the door. He looked tired and sad.

"You miss her, don't you?" I said.

"Pin sweel Heartfoot," Uncle Arvie said.

"I didn't much like that Colin guy, did you?"

"Beany booger!"

"Exactly," I said. "A right old beany booger."

We were nearly home when Uncle Arvie said, "Two please?"

I had nearly forgotten about the three pleases. I had done the first please, by finding the book with its letter and giving it to Aunt Julia. Now what would the next please be?

CHAPTER FIVE

The Second Please

As we were crossing the park on our way home from Aunt Julia's, a boy on a bike stopped us. The bike was spectacular, but the boy was not. It was Billy Baker, the one who had once called me a liar when I had told him about my ghosts.

Billy Baker said, "Hey, stupid Danny. Is that your stupid stinking dog?"

Bo growled a long, low, menacing growl.

"It's my dog," I said, "but he's not stupid or stinking."

"Oh yeah?" Billy said. "I bet he is."

"Beany booger?" Uncle Arvie said.

"Yes," I agreed. "A beany booger."

"What?" Billy demanded. "Who are you calling a 'beany booger'?"

"Nobody."

Billy grabbed my collar. "You'd better not be calling *me* a 'beany booger', that's all I can say."

Bo grasped Billy's trousers in his teeth and pulled at them.

"Hey, get your stupid stinking dog off me!"

"You shouldn't have called him stupid or stinking," I said.

Bo pulled at Billy's trousers, making him lose his balance. Billy fell off his bike.

"Get this dog off me!"

"Come on, Bo. Let him go."

Reluctantly, Bo let Billy loose. As Billy rode away, he shouted, "You'll be sorry for this! I'll catch you sometime when you don't have your stupid stinking dog or that stinking old man to protect you."

What? I thought. Had Billy Baker actually *seen* Uncle Arvie?

"Beany booger," Uncle Arvie said again.

"Exactly," I agreed. "He likes to cause trouble."

Back in my room, Uncle Arvie again mentioned the second "please" as he rummaged in my desk.

"What are you looking for?" I asked.

"Hammertoe." Uncle Arvie pulled out pencils and pens, paper and a ruler. "Nod hammertoe?"

"I don't know. What exactly is a hammertoe?"

"Hammertoe!" Uncle Arvie moved his hand in the air. "Hammer a needle. With hammertoe and needlinks."

I had absolutely no idea what he was talking about.

Suddenly, he shouted, "Ha! Hammertoe!"

"A *paintbrush*?"

"Hammertoe! Yin!" Uncle Arvie said. "Hammertoe. Hammer a needle." He clapped his hands and rummaged some more. He pulled out a twisted tube of blue oil paint from my desk. "Needlinks! Hammer a needle with needlinks!"

"You want me to paint a picture with the brush and paint?" I guessed.

"Pin needle. Dinosaur flannelate," Uncle Arvie explained.

"*Your* picture? You want me to – to – what?"

"Flannelate!" Uncle Arvie was frustrated. He didn't know how to explain.

"Can't you show me?" I asked. "With the paintbrush and the paint?"

Uncle Arvie thought for a minute. He took a piece of paper and placed it on the desk. Next he opened the paint tube and squeezed a drop on to the paper. He dipped the brush in the paint and started to draw, but an odd thing happened. There was paint on the brush, and the brush was moving across the paper, but the brush was leaving no marks.

"Golly," I said. "Is it invisible paint?"

Uncle Arvie slammed his fist on the desk. "Nod fraggle." He dropped the brush and covered his face with his hands.

"Let me try." I dipped the brush in the paint and stroked it across the paper. "Look, it works for me." I painted a thin blue line across the paper, added a few strokes, and drew a house.

Uncle Arvie tapped at the picture. "Dinosaur needle." He jumped up, took the paint brush, and pretended to paint a picture in the air. "Pin needle." Then he dropped the brush. "Nod flannelate."

"Not *finished*? Is that it? Your painting isn't finished?" I asked.

"Yin, riggle! Dinosaur flannelate!" Uncle Arvie shouted.

"Wait a minute," I said. "Let me get this straight. You've got a painting – an unfinished painting – and you want *me* to finish it?"

"Riggle!"

"I can't do that," I said. "I don't know how to paint."

Uncle Arvie held up my drawing of the house. "Dinosaur hammer," Uncle Arvie begged.

"Where *is* your painting?" I asked.

Uncle Arvie shrugged. He wasn't sure.

"Well, I guess we'll go back to your house tomorrow and see if we can find it. But I don't guarantee anything. Like I told you, I really don't know how to paint."

Uncle Arvie looked relieved. He cleared the top of the desk. "Stamp!" he said, and he lay down on the desk and fell asleep. Bo curled up at the foot of the desk and he, too, fell asleep.

Uncle Arvie slept all day, and I was glad. It was very hard keeping up with a ghost who used such unusual words and asked for favours. I wondered where his painting was and how hard it would be to finish it.

That night, as I lay in bed, I remembered something. Billy Baker had said something about the "old man". If Billy really had seen Uncle Arvie, then Billy, too, had seen a ghost. Wouldn't Billy be surprised to know that?

I stared out of the window and searched the sky for a bright star. When I found one, I wished for my *pepperoni*.

CHAPTER SIX

Hammering the Needle

On Sunday morning, I heard, "Dinosaur?" There was Uncle Arvie, floating near the ceiling again. "Good carpet, Dinosaur!"

"Good morning." I could smell pancakes and it occurred to me that I hadn't seen Uncle Arvie eat since he had arrived. "Aren't you hungry?" I asked him.

"Nod."

"Do ghosts eat?"

"Nod."

"What do you do all day – when you're not visiting me, I mean? You don't eat. What do you do?"

"Stamp."

"Sleep? Is that all?"

"Nod." Uncle Arvie flapped his arms. "Mailer."

"Sleep and fly. I'd like that. Can you go wherever you want?"

"Nod." Uncle Arvie wiggled his arms and twirled and fell over. "Pailandplop."

"Oh, right. You can't steer. You mean you just have to go where the wind takes you?"

"Yin."

Maybe that was why my father had not come to see me yet. Maybe he couldn't find his way.

"Danny?" my mother called. She tapped at the door and came in. "You awake?"

Uncle Arvie smiled at her. "Feather macaroni."

"What *is* that smell?" my mother said. "It's so *familiar*, and yet—"

"Does it remind you of someone?" I asked.

"Yes, I think it does, but I can't exactly say who . . ."

Uncle Arvie jumped up and down. "Pin!" he said. "Pin! Pin!"

"So what are you and Bo doing today?" my mother asked.

"Hammer a needle!" Uncle Arvie said. "Dinosaur flannelete!"

"I thought maybe we'd go over to Aunt Julia's for a while," I said.

"She must be very lonely now that Arvie is gone."

Uncle Arvie looked sad. "Pin Heartfoot. Pin sweel."

"I bet he's lonely too," I said.

My mother looked surprised. "But Danny, he's in heaven. He won't be lonely."

"Maybe you don't stay in heaven all the time," I said. "Maybe sometimes you ride around on the wind all by yourself and—"

"Danny, what an imagination you have!"

"Do you think my pepperoni is lonely?"

"Your *what*?"

"I – I meant my father. Dad. Do you think he's lonely?"

My mother sat down on the bed beside me. "I don't know for sure, but no, I don't think he's lonely."

"I hope not," I said. "I hope he isn't lonely, but I bet he does miss us."

"I'm sure he does, Danny." She stared at her wedding ring. "I miss him *terribly*. Most of the time I'm too busy to be lonely, but at night . . ."

"I know," I said. "At night it's harder."

After breakfast, Uncle Arvie dusted off his boots and straightened his hat. "Pin mailer," he said, and he waggled his arms, lifted a few inches off the floor, and then came back down again. "Foomf!" he said. He waggled his arms again. Nothing happened. "Foomf!" Again he tried, and this time, he lifted smoothly into the air and sailed through the window and over the trees, settling down in the grass across the road. At least he could steer for short distances, it seemed.

Aunt Julia was surprised to see me and Bo again. "I do so love to have company," she said.

"Pin Heartfoot," Uncle Arvie sighed.

I asked to use the toilet. I knew the painting would not be *there*, but it would give me a chance to look in the bedrooms. I'd have to be quiet and quick about it, though.

I heard Aunt Julia in the kitchen. Quickly, I went into the spare bedroom and looked under the bed, behind the wardrobe and in the closet. No paintings, except for the one on the wall that looked completely finished.

In Aunt Julia's bedroom, I checked under the bed and in the closet. I felt terrible, like a spy.

"Danny?" Aunt Julia called.

I hurried back down the hallway to the kitchen.

"I thought maybe you got lost," she laughed.

I had an idea. "One time when I was here, I think I left something in your garage." I had to think fast. "Remember those little plastic dinosaurs I had? Do you think I could check if I left them here?"

"Your dinosaurs? I don't remember seeing them out there," she said. "But you can go look."

The garage was stacked with boxes, gardening tools, an old bicycle, rubbish bins and paint cans. When I asked Uncle Arvie how big the painting was, he held out his arms to show how wide and then swivelled them to show how tall.

"That's a pretty big painting," I said. "We shouldn't miss something that big." I poked around the boxes, moved tools, and searched the rafters. "It's not here. Can you think of anywhere else it could be?"

Uncle Arvie scratched his head. Suddenly he said, "Picket!" and pointed to the roof.

"I don't think a painting is going to be on the roof—"

Uncle Arvie pointed towards the house and then towards the roof. "Picket! Picket!"

"The *attic*?"

"Riggle! Picket!"

"Did you find your dinosaurs?" Aunt Julia called.

"No, I must have left them somewhere else." I was trying to think of a way to get into the attic. "Do you want me to do anything for you while I'm here?"

"Well, isn't that sweet of you," she said. "I can't think of anything—"

"Do you need anything taken up to the attic?"

"The attic? My goodness. I haven't been up there in *years*. I'm sure it's a complete mess. No, I don't think I need anything carried up there, though."

Uncle Arvie was sitting beside her, staring at her with a smile on his face. He liked to watch her.

"Maybe I could go up there and straighten it up for you," I said. When I said this, I felt a bit guilty, because my own mother had asked me to clean *our* attic, and I was always finding excuses not to do it. "I like to poke around in attics," I added.

"What a lovely boy," she said. "If you're sure you want to, it's fine with me. Here, I'll show you where the ladder is."

The attic was dusty and crowded with boxes, old suitcases, a trunk, cast-off pieces of furniture, and plastic sacks filled with blankets and clothing.

"I'll be down in the kitchen if you need me," Aunt Julia said from the foot of the ladder. Bo stared up at the hole through which Uncle Arvie and I had disappeared. He whimpered.

I moved boxes, clearing a space in the middle of the attic. "I might as well straighten it up as I go," I said. I made a neat stack of boxes, and piled the furniture against one wall. Then I dragged the plastic sacks across the room and piled them on top of the furniture.

"I don't suppose you'd like to *help* me?" I asked.

"Nod middle." Uncle Arvie tried to lift a box, but his hands went right through it.

"But you picked up a book – and a photograph—"

"Peasy!" He picked up a crumpled piece of paper and tossed it in the air. Then he kicked a tennis ball across the room. "Peasy!" But when he tried to move one of the suitcases, he couldn't.

41

"Too heavy?" I said.

"Yin."

So I moved the suitcases. They weren't *that* heavy, since they were empty. All, that is, except for the last one.

"Hey, something's in this one."

Uncle Arvie shouted, "Needle! Pin needle!"

Hurriedly, I unzipped the suitcase. Inside was a flat wooden box and a large object wrapped in brown paper.

"Needle! Pin needle!" Uncle Arvie said.

I tore the paper off the object and sure enough, inside was a large canvas. It was a beautiful painting of a blue sky with white puffy clouds, a blue-green lake, and rolling green hills. In the middle of the lake was a row-boat with two people in it. A lady was sitting in the front, and a man was rowing.

But the painting was unfinished, just as Uncle Arvie had said. On the right side of the painting, in the lower corner, was a patch of white canvas. It looked as if there should be another hill there, or more of the lake.

Uncle Arvie touched the people in the boat. "Pin and Heartfoot," he said.

It did look like Uncle Arvie and Aunt Julia in the boat. "Wow, I wish I could paint like that."

"Dinosaur hammer," Uncle Arvie said.

"I don't know. I could never paint this well. Is this a real place?"

"Bunny room," Uncle Arvie said.

"It doesn't much look like a bunny room to me."

"Bunny room! Pin and Heartfoot. Bunny room!" He made kissing sounds with his mouth and showed me the gold ring on his finger.

"Honeymoon! This is where you went on your honeymoon, isn't it?"

"Yin, yin, yin! Bunny room!"

In the wooden box that was also in the suitcase, I found tubes of paint and paintbrushes. "Well, let's give it a try. What goes in this unfinished corner?"

Uncle Arvie touched a hill and a tree. He showed me how to mix two shades of green and one shade of yellow to get the right colour. I worked slowly. I wanted it to look just right.

The grassy hill was fairly easy, but my tree looked sick. Uncle Arvie added some black paint to the brown that I was using, and very, very lightly, he placed his hand on top of mine, guiding my fingers slowly across the canvas.

"Wow," I said when he had finished. "It looks like a real tree! I can paint! Well, with a bit of help. Now I guess it has to dry a while, huh?"

Uncle Arvie held up three fingers and pushed one back down.

"Two hours?"

"Donkeys," Uncle Arvie said, waving his fingers. "Donkeys."

"Days?"

"Riggle! Donkeys!"

"Two whole days? That's a long time." I leaned the painting against the wall and dragged a box in front of it, to hide it but not touch it. "Is this for Aunt Julia? A present for her?"

"Yin. Pin needle a Heartfoot. Bunny room."

"She'll like it, I bet."

We heard the doorbell ring below, and then voices. Uncle Arvie listened carefully. Suddenly he flew down through the attic opening. "Beany booger!" he said.

CHAPTER SEVEN
Beany Booger

Downstairs, Aunt Julia was saying, "Oh, how lovely. I do so love chocolates." She held a box of candy, and beside her stood Colin, smiling his silvery smile. Uncle Arvie stamped his foot, and Bo growled. "Would anyone like some tea?" she said, heading for the kitchen. "Come on, Colin, I know you'd love a cup of tea."

Uncle Arvie glared as Colin followed her down the hall. Aunt Julia asked Colin to open the box of chocolates while she prepared the tea. Bo circled Colin, sniffing at his legs and growling.

"Shoo," Colin said. "Go away, dog."

"His name is Bo," I said.

Colin opened the chocolates and put the box on the table. Uncle Arvie leaned close. "Beany booger," he said, as he reached in and pressed his fingers into five of the chocolates, crushing them.

Aunt Julia said, "Let me see those chocolates.

I do so love choc— oh!" She stared down at the crushed candy.

Colin bent to look at the chocolates, too. "Hey," he said, blushing.

"Oh, never mind," Aunt Julia said. "I'm sure the others are fine." She and Colin smiled at each other.

Uncle Arvie reached into the box and crushed five more chocolates.

"I'll have one of the others," Aunt Julia said, putting her hand into the box. "Ack—!" she said, seeing the mashed candy.

"Hey," Colin said to me. "Did you—"

"I didn't touch them," I said, holding up my clean fingers as proof. "And neither did Bo. He hates candy."

Uncle Arvie pinched Colin's arm.

"Hey!" Colin shouted, slapping at his sleeve. "Hey!"

"Oh dear," Aunt Julia said, "not another wasp?"

Uncle Arvie pinched Colin's neck.

"Hey!" Colin slapped wildly at his neck and arms. "I gotta go!" He rushed to the door.

"Bye, beany bud booger," Uncle Arvie said.

"Goodness," Aunt Julia said. "I'll have to do something about those wasps." She picked up the box of candy, looked sadly at it, and threw it in the bin.

Uncle Arvie seemed rather pleased.

"Did you finish cleaning the attic?" Aunt Julia asked.

"Not completely," I said, knowing we needed to wait two days for the painting to dry. "I'll come back on Tuesday and finish, OK?"

"You're such a lovely boy," she sighed.

When Uncle Arvie, Bo and I reached the park across from my house, Uncle Arvie said, "Mailer. Pin mailer." He flapped his arms, rose up in the air a few inches, and fell back to the ground. "Foomf."

"I guess it isn't always so easy," I said.

Uncle Arvie waggled his arms. Up he rose. He put one hand on his red cowboy hat to hold it on. He wobbled and flipped and rose far into the air.

"Be careful!" I shouted. "Don't get caught in the wind!"

Uncle Arvie somersaulted in the air. "Oowee!" he said. He flipped and turned and finally floated down until he was level with my window. Quickly, he flapped his arms, and in through my window he sailed.

Bo barked, and at first I thought he was barking at Uncle Arvie's flying. Then I realized he was barking at someone else. Billy Baker was riding towards me on his bike.

I wished I had a bike like Billy's. I'd asked for one for my birthday last year, but my mother said she couldn't afford one. I had started saving my pocket money for one, but at the rate that was adding up, I'd be too old for a bike by the time I had enough money for one.

"Keep that stupid stinking dog away from me," Billy called as he spun around us. "Where's the old geezer?"

"What old geezer?"

"That old geezer in the stupid red hat. That old geezer who was with you yesterday."

"He's not an old geezer," I said.

"Oh yeah? Well, he looked like a stupid old geezer to me," Billy said.

"He's a ghost."

Billy laughed a wicked laugh. "Sure he was, and I'm a piece of lettuce!" Billy grabbed my arm and squeezed it hard. "You stupid liar."

"He *is* a ghost," I insisted. My arm hurt like crazy.

Bo grabbed Billy's shoelace and pulled at it.

"Get off," Billy said, kicking at Bo. "Get this stupid stinking dog off me."

"I'll get him off if you let go of my arm and listen to me for a minute."

"Get the dog off first," Billy said.

"No, you let go of my arm first."

Billy let go, and I pulled Bo away.

"You've got one minute," Billy said. "Talk. And it better be good."

"It *was* a ghost you saw, and I can prove it," I said.

"Right. This I've gotta see."

"See that house over there?" I said. "The ghost is in there right now. See that window up there? You wait here and watch. I'm going to ask the ghost to fly out of that window. Then will you believe me?"

"What do you think I am?" Billy said. "Some kind of idiot?"

"Just wait. You'll see." I raced across the street, with Bo following me. Now I'd show Billy Baker once and for all that there *was* such a thing as a ghost.

I ran upstairs. "Uncle Arvie, Uncle Arvie." I flung open my bedroom door and there was Uncle Arvie, lying across my desk, sound asleep and snoring.

Outside, Billy Baker stared up at my window. I shook Uncle Arvie. "Wake up! Please wake up!" I shook him and wobbled him and pulled on his arm. "Please, please wake up," I begged.

Billy stared up at the window, waiting. I patted Uncle Arvie's face and tickled his chin. "Please, please, please, wake up!" But no matter what I did, I could not wake him.

I saw Billy pick up a rock and hold it in his hand. "Please, please, please," I begged Uncle Arvie. Uncle Arvie snored. At last I said, "Come on, Bo," and went outside.

Billy tossed the rock up and down in his hand. "So where's the stupid ghost?" he said.

"He's asleep."

"Ha, ha, ha!" Billy laughed wickedly. "Man, you are more stupid than I thought. The ghost is *asleep*! Oh man, oh man. How about if I throw this rock through that window up there and wake him up? Huh?"

Bo growled.

"Look," I said. "Really. I can prove he's a ghost. Meet me here tomorrow after school. I'm sure I can get him to fly then."

"Man, oh man, oh man," Billy said. "I don't believe this. You must think I am stupider than you."

"Really," I said. "I *promise*."

Bo growled and snapped at Billy's shoe.

"Okay," Billy said quickly. "I'll give you one more chance. Tomorrow after school. Right here. And that stupid old geezer ghost better fly or you're going to see this here rock fly – right through your stupid old window." Off rode Billy, still tossing the rock in one hand.

I sure hoped Uncle Arvie would fly for Billy. I sure hoped he would.

CHAPTER EIGHT
Nod Mailer

On Monday after school, I dashed home, where Bo leaped on me, plastering my clothes with sloppy drools. My mother was still at work. "Come on, Bo," I said. "Let's get Uncle Arvie."

I was relieved to find Uncle Arvie awake. He was sitting on my desk holding a picture of his wife. "Pin sweel Heartfoot," Uncle Arvie sighed.

Through the window, I saw Billy Baker riding his bike across the park, towards the spot where we had agreed to meet. "Uncle Arvie, I have a favour to ask," I said.

"A please?"

"Yes. I want you to show Billy Baker that you know how to fly."

"Pin mailer!" Uncle Arvie shouted, flapping his arms.

"Not yet," I said, and I led Uncle Arvie downstairs and across the street.

Billy Baker sat on his bike, his arms crossed

over his chest. "So let's see this old geezer fly," he said. "I don't have all day, you know."

"Pin mailer?" Uncle Arvie said.

"What's he talking about?" Billy asked. "What's a *pin mailer*?"

"You'll see," I said. "Uncle Arvie, go ahead. Show him. Fly."

Uncle Arvie straightened his cowboy hat and stretched his arms. He flapped them once, twice, three times. "Foomf!" he said. Again he flapped his arms, this time faster. Once, twice, three times. "Foomf!"

Billy said, "Oh man, oh man, oh man. Just as I thought."

"Wait," I said. "Sometimes it takes a while for him to warm up."

Billy looked at his watch. "Like I said, I don't have all day. He'd better hurry."

Uncle Arvie tried again. He wiggled and wobbled his arms. He flapped them up and down. He waved them all around. He turned in circles. "Foomf! Foomf!" he grunted.

Nothing happened.

"Stupid geezer," Billy said. "Stupid dog. Stupid kid." He circled us on his bike. "Man oh man, are you gonna be sorry," he said, and he rode off.

Uncle Arvie frowned. "Nod mailer."

"The one time I ask you to do something," I said, "the one time I need you to fly, and what happens?"

"Nod mailer." He looked pitiful.

Across the street, my mother was getting off the bus. "Hi!" she called. "How was your day?"

"Terrible, just terrible."

"That bad? Well, come on in, and tell me about it."

From the kitchen we heard a crash and a thud upstairs. In my bedroom, we discovered the shattered window and, on the floor, a rock. Pieces of glass covered the carpet.

"Oh!" my mother said, looking out of the window. "Who would do such a nasty thing?"

"Beany bud booger," Uncle Arvie said.

I wanted to tell her who had done it, but if I did, she might call Billy's parents. And then he might do something much worse. "Maybe it was an accident," I said.

"Let's hope so," she said, but she didn't seem convinced.

CHAPTER NINE
Needle for Heartfoot

On Tuesday, we returned to Aunt Julia's house. She was just coming home from work and must have stopped for groceries on the way home, because she was loaded down with carrier bags.

"Thank you," she said, as I took the bags from her. "I wasn't sure that you'd really come today. I thought you might forget."

She put her groceries away and sank on to the sofa. "I'm a little tired," she said. "I hope you don't mind if I put my feet up and take a little nap while you putter around in the attic."

Uncle Arvie gazed at his wife. "Pin lalley, pin sweel, pin Heartfoot."

In the attic, I hurriedly pulled the painting from its hiding place and touched the portion of the canvas which I'd painted. "It feels dry to me. How does it look?"

Uncle Arvie stepped back and studied the painting. "Bunny room needle a Heartfoot! Feather bunny room!"

"You like it?"

"Feather, feather bunny room!"

"Don't you need to sign it or something?" I asked.

Uncle Arvie held up his arms. "Nod fraggle—"

"Oh right," I said. "I suppose I could sign it for you, but then it would have to dry again." I smoothed out the brown paper which had originally covered the canvas. "Let's write something on the paper instead." I held my hand over the paper as Uncle Arvie guided me. *Pin Heartfoot*, we wrote.

"I'll just finish tidying up, and then I'll give it to her, OK? That's what I'm supposed to do, isn't it? Give it to her?"

"Yin, riggle!" Uncle Arvie was as excited as a child at Christmas.

I finished stacking furniture and boxes against the wall, swept the room, and dropped a sack of rubbish down through the attic opening. Carefully, I eased the painting down through the hatch.

Aunt Julia was dozing on the sofa. I patted her arm. "Aunt Julia?"

"Oh!" she said. "Goodness, I was in dreamland! Are you finished already?"

"Yes," I said. "And I found something. I thought maybe it was for you. I didn't mean to be nosy. When I moved a suitcase, I heard this clunking sound, and I just thought I'd look. This was inside. See? It says *Pin Heartfoot* on it."

Aunt Julia sat up quickly and put her hands to her mouth. "What on earth . . .?" She ran her fingers lightly over the words *Pin Heartfoot*. "It's from Arvie."

Uncle Arvie sat beside her on the sofa.

"You haven't seen it before?" I asked.

"No, I haven't. What can it be?" She turned the package over and unsealed the edges of the paper.

Beside her, Uncle Arvie was grinning, and Bo thumped his tail eagerly.

Aunt Julia pulled the paper away and held the canvas in front of her. "Oh, oh, oh," she said. "Oh, oh, oh. Goodness, goodness, goodness." She was crying. "It's our honeymoon. There's that beautiful lake, and look, there we are in the boat. That's me, and that's – oh, that's my Arvie."

She covered her face in her hands. Beside her, Uncle Arvie's lip quivered.

"Do you like it?" I asked.

Aunt Julia sniffled. "Oh yes. Oh yes, I do." She stared at the painting. "I bet this was supposed to be my birthday present. I bet he hid it in the attic, and then . . . oh my Arvie."

Uncle Arvie leaned over and kissed her cheek, and immediately she put her hand to her face. "Oh! I can almost *feel* him here with us right now." She sniffed the air. "Do you know – I can almost *smell* him here!" She laughed. "I bet you think I'm crazy, don't you?"

"No," I said. "Not a bit."

CHAPTER TEN
The Third Please

When we returned home after giving the painting to Aunt Julia, my mother was taping a piece of cardboard over a second window. "Another rock," she explained, showing us the glass on the carpet. "I've had enough of this. I'm going to find out who's doing such a horrid thing."

Later, I said to Uncle Arvie, "We've got to do something about Billy. He doesn't seem to care if he gets caught – which makes me think he's got something worse up his sleeve."

"Pin mailer," Uncle Arvie suggested.

"If only you could fly when I really *need* you to fly."

Uncle Arvie yawned. "Stamp!" He lay down across my desk. Within minutes, he was snoring.

I stretched out on my bed and looked at the cloudy sky. I closed my eyes and imagined a clear sky with a single bright star, and on it I wished for my *pepperoni*.

I was awakened early the next morning by

Uncle Arvie. "Good carpet, Dinosaur! Good carpet! Three please?"

There was a third favour to do for Uncle Arvie. "I've got school today," I said. "So it will have to be when I get home. What's the third please?"

"Dunder trampolink. Dunder boodled trampolink a gressapip."

"Hold on a minute!"

Uncle Arvie got down on his knees and scratched at the carpet. "Dunder," he said. "Dunder, dunder, dunder."

"You want me to clean the carpet?"

"Nod!" He pawed at the floor.

"You want me to dig something?"

"Yin! Yin! Dinosaur dunder!"

"Why?"

"Trampolink boodled. A gressapip." Uncle Arvie pretended to dig in the carpet. Suddenly, he stopped. He stared down at the carpet. "Trampolink!" he shouted. "Boodled trampolink!"

"I haven't a clue what you're talking about, and I'm late for school."

"Nod dunder?"

"OK, OK, I'll dig for you, I guess. But I have

no idea what I'm digging for or where I'll be digging. Can you explain to me after school?"

"Yin! Dinosaur dunder! Dinosaur dunder!"

At school that day, Billy Baker grabbed me in the hall. "That'll teach you to tell your stupid stories about stupid ghosts."

"Let go," I said, struggling against Billy's strong grip. "You wouldn't be so brave if your father knew about those rocks—"

"Oh yeah?" he said. "My father's *dead*. So there."

"Dead?"

"Yeah, dead. Now admit it: the old geezer is not a ghost. The old geezer is an old geezer."

I struggled. "He *is* a ghost."

Billy socked me hard on the arm. "Man oh man oh man. Don't you ever learn? You'd better be in the park today at four o'clock. The old geezer better fly then or you won't have a single window left in your house, got it?"

"I can't be there at four. I've got to dunder – I've got something to do." Billy squeezed my arm. "But I'll be there at six," I said.

Billy breathed in my face. "Yeah? Six? OK, six o'clock, stupid."

All day long, I prayed that Uncle Arvie would be able to fly that night at six o'clock, and all day long I wondered why Billy could see my ghost, but no one else could.

After school, Uncle Arvie and Bo were waiting for me at the door of my house. "Dunder!" Uncle Arvie said.

On down the road we went. I hoped it would not take too long. I hoped we'd be finished by six o'clock. I was not surprised to discover that we were headed for Aunt Julia's house again, but I was surprised to see, as we neared the house, someone leaving a box on the front steps.

Bo growled and Uncle Arvie clenched his fists when he recognized Colin.

"I was just leaving this for Julia," Colin said. "She's not home."

"I know," I said. "I'm going to – to weed the garden for her."

Uncle Arvie crept slowly up to Colin.

"Will you tell her I left this for her?" Colin said. "It's another box of chocolates. I'm sure *these* aren't smashed. I can't imagine what happened to those others. And I can't imagine why

I keep getting stung by wasps when I'm here."
He looked around quickly. "Do you see any?"

"Any what?" I said.

"Any wasps?"

"Well," I said, as Uncle Arvie reached for Colin's arm. "As a matter of fact—"

"Ow! Hey! Ow!" Colin shouted, slapping at his arm. He ran down the path and dived into his car.

"Beany booger," Uncle Arvie said, kicking the chocolates into the bushes and heading for the garage. "Beany, beany bud booger."

While Uncle Arvie rummaged in the garage, I examined the old rusty bicycle I'd seen earlier, when we'd been looking for Uncle Arvie's painting. I wondered if maybe I could fix the bicycle. But the more I looked at it, the more things I saw wrong with it. It was covered in rust. Both tyres were flat. The chain was hanging loose. One pedal was missing. The handlebars were bent.

"Dinosaur!" Uncle Arvie called. He had found a spade, which apparently was what he had been looking for. He motioned for me to bring the spade, and out to the back garden he marched. He walked slowly around, scratching his head. "Gressapip," he said, waving his arm across the bushes and flowers.

"Garden?"

"Yin, riggle! Gressapip!" Uncle Arvie continued walking around the flowers. At last he stopped in front of a rose bush. "Dunder!"

Bo tilted his head from one side to the other and whimpered.

"Here? You want me to dig up Aunt Julia's rose bush? Won't she be mad?"

"Dunder trampolink. Boodled trampolink a gressapip." Uncle Arvie jumped up and down and held his arms wide. "Trampolink! Boodled trampolink a gressapip!"

"OK, OK, OK," I said. "I'll dunder the trampolink – whatever that is – here in the gressapip. But Aunt Julia's not going to like it when she sees her rose bush all dug up."

With his finger, Uncle Arvie drew a large circle around the rose bush. Apparently he wanted me to dig all the way around the bush so I wouldn't chop its roots. I dug and dug, and all the while I kept an eye on my watch. I hoped we'd be finished by six o'clock.

CHAPTER ELEVEN
Dundering Trampolink

For half an hour, I dug. The rose bush was now lying beside the hole. Bo and Uncle Ärvie were sitting on the grass watching me.

"Are you sure I'm digging in the right place?"

Uncle Arvie scratched his head.

"Can't *you* dig a while?"

"Nod. Nod dunder." Uncle Arvie pushed the spade against the ground with all his strength. It didn't even make a dent in the earth.

"Ghosts sure are peculiar," I said. "You can fly, but you can't dig. You can pinch, but you can't paint or write. You can lift little things, but not big ones. Very weird."

Bo jumped into the hole. He scratched at the ground with his paws, sending clumps of earth flying into the air.

"Elephant dunder!" Uncle Arvie said.

"Good old Bo, you're a good old digger."

"Danny? Is that you?" It was Aunt Julia, home from work.

"Uh oh," I said. "Now we're in trouble."

Aunt Julia walked towards me. "What in the world . . . ? What *are* you doing? Oh my goodness!" She stared at her toppled rose bush and at the hole in which Bo was digging. "Danny, I hope you have an explanation for this."

I thought. "Well, I . . ." I thought some more. "I had this dream . . ."

"What sort of dream?"

"In this dream, I saw Uncle Arvie—"

Aunt Julia gasped. "*My* Arvie?"

"Yes, and he told me to dunder up the gressapip – and that seemed to mean I should dig up the garden, right here."

"Under my favourite rose bush?"

"Well, yes," I admitted.

"Do you know why it's my favourite rose bush?" she asked.

"No."

"It's because it was a present from Arvie. He planted it here with his own hands, three years ago."

"Oh. I'm sorry I dug it up," I said, glaring at Uncle Arvie, who was sitting on the grass

69

watching her. Bo was still scratching away at the hole, flinging earth.

"I don't understand why you would have a dream about Arvie telling you to dig up my favourite rose bush. Have you been eating too much candy lately?" she asked.

Bo barked. He leaped out of the hole and pulled at my trousers.

"What is it?" I asked. "Quit pulling me." Bo barked and leaped back into the hole. He scratched at the earth.

"Wait a minute," Aunt Julia said. "What's that?"

In the middle of the hole was a piece of green metal. I reached in and brushed away the earth, uncovering more green metal and a brass handle. "It looks like some sort of box," I said. With the spade, I loosened the earth around the box.

"It *is* a box," Aunt Julia said.

I slipped the spade beneath the box and lifted it out of the hole. It was not a very big box, but it was heavy.

"Trampolink!" Uncle Arvie said. "Boodled trampolink!"

"Buried treasure?" I said.

"Riggle!"

"Is it locked?" Aunt Julia asked.

I brushed the earth away. There was a small brass latch at the front, and it wasn't locked.

CHAPTER TWELVE
Boodling Chinkapink

"I feel very peculiar," Aunt Julia said, sinking to the grass. She sniffed the air. "This is very strange. Very, very strange. You'd better open the box, Danny. I can't."

Inside the box was a bundle of letters tied with brown string. "What on earth . . . ?" she said. She touched the top letter. "These are letters I wrote to Arvie before we were married. He *saved* them?" She lifted the bundle from the box, and as she did so, she revealed what was beneath the letters.

"Trampolink!" Uncle Arvie said.

Beneath the letters were bundles of old notes and bags of coins.

"Money!" I said. "Treasure! Trampolink!"

"Why, look at all this money," Aunt Julia said. "Hundreds, thousands . . ." She covered her face with her hands.

"Don't cry," I said. "I'm sure he didn't steal it."

"That's not why I'm crying. I *know* Arvie didn't steal this. He saved it. For years and years and years."

"But why didn't he put it in the bank?" I asked.

"Arvie? Put money in a *bank*? He didn't believe in banks," she said. "After he died, I found little bits of money hidden everywhere – in his shoes, in his jackets, in our wardrobe. I knew there had to be more money somewhere, but I had no idea where. And I had no idea it was this much! Just think, if you hadn't had that dream . . ."

She picked up the letters and the box full of money. "I'll take these inside," she said. "What a miracle! I'm going to call your mother and tell her what you've found. Goodness, goodness, goodness!"

As I started re-filling the hole with earth, Uncle Arvie said, "Boodle chinkapink?" He and Bo ran across the grass and towards the front of the house. When they reappeared, Bo was carrying the box of chocolates which Colin had brought earlier. "Boodle the chinkapink!" Uncle Arvie said. Bo obeyed by dropping the box of candy into the hole.

"OK, boodle the chinkapink!" I said. I covered the box of chocolates with earth, replaced the rose bush on top of it, and spread more earth around the bush. "Maybe it will grow chocolate flowers."

"Chinkapink in the gressapip!" Uncle Arvie said.

On the way home, I felt terrific. It had been exciting to find the buried treasure, and Aunt Julia seemed so happy. She hadn't even counted the money yet. She seemed more excited at finding the letters, and when I had left her, she was sitting at the kitchen table reading them.

As we neared home, Uncle Arvie said, "Pin mailer?"

Without thinking, I said, "Sure, go ahead."

Uncle Arvie wiggled his arms and flew into the air and away.

"Oh no!" I cried. "Wait!" I looked at my watch. It was almost six o'clock. Billy would be waiting.

CHAPTER THIRTEEN
Mailer, Mailer

A strong wind was blowing through the park when I reached it. Leaves whipped through the air. I wondered if I had time to go home first and get Uncle Arvie. I was afraid Uncle Arvie would go to sleep again, and I wouldn't be able to wake him.

But it was too late. Billy Baker was riding towards me, pedalling fast, and he looked angry. He squealed to a stop and jumped off his bike. "Man oh man, it sure is windy," he said. The wind blew his hair in wild tangles, making him look even more threatening. He grabbed my collar and snarled, "So where's the old geezer, you stupid kid?"

I strained to look across the road at my house. I thought I saw something move in the window upstairs. Was it Uncle Arvie?

Billy threw me to the ground and knelt on my chest. "Repeat after me: 'The old geezer is an old geezer.'" Billy's hands pressed against my arms.

"He isn't," I said. "He isn't an old geezer."

Billy twisted my wrists. "Repeat after me: 'The old geezer is an old geezer.' "

I squirmed and twisted, trying to get loose. A flicker of red flashed in the air above us. "Look – up there—"

"Don't try to pull that one on me," Billy said. "You're just trying to distract me."

"Really, look, up there—"

Billy turned quickly. "Where?"

"There, above the road – coming this way."

Billy gasped. "Geez . . ."

Uncle Arvie was flying.

"Holy moly," Billy said.

I twisted beneath him and rolled free.

The wind whipped the leaves through the air, and Uncle Arvie rose and somersaulted and dived and soared. "Oowee!" Uncle Arvie shouted. "Mailer! Mailer! Oowee!" Uncle Arvie twisted and turned and looped.

"H-h-holy m-m-moly!" Billy cried. He crouched in the grass, covering his head with his arms. "Get that thing away from me," he whimpered.

Uncle Arvie dived and swept past Billy's face.

"H-h-holy m-m-moly," Billy moaned.

"He's a ghost," I said. "Say it. Say, 'He's not an old geezer. He's a ghost.' "

Uncle Arvie flew above the tree and dived again, narrowly missing Billy's head.

"Say it."

"OK, OK," Billy said. "He's not an old geezer. He's a g-g-ghost. Now make him stop!"

A strong blast of wind blew through the park. "Oowee," Uncle Arvie said, as the wind caught him and carried him far into the air. "Pailandplop!" he shouted. "Pailandplop!"

"Uh-oh," I said, watching Uncle Arvie rise higher and higher. "He can't steer."

Billy peeked from between his fingers at the sight of Uncle Arvie flying higher and higher into the sky. "Where's he going?" Billy asked.

"Pailandplop, pailandplop!" Uncle Arvie shouted, but his voice was fainter and fainter as he sailed towards the clouds.

"Come back," I shouted. "Come back." I ran across the park, following Uncle Arvie, trying to keep him in sight.

A thin echo drifted down: "Pailandplop—"

"Oh please," I called. "Try! Try to steer!"

But the wind was too strong. It pulled Uncle Arvie up into the clouds, and I could see him no more. I stood for a long time watching the sky, hoping to see that red cowboy hat.

There was nothing more to be seen. Uncle Arvie was gone.

I walked back across the park, passing Billy, who was still crouched on the grass. "Wait . . ." Billy called.

I kept walking.

My mother and Bo were standing in the back garden. "Danny!" my mother said. "Where have you been? Aunt Julia called and – what's wrong? Is something the matter?"

I looked up into the sky once more and then I knelt beside Bo. I whispered in Bo's ear: "Uncle Arvie flew away."

Bo cocked his head and whimpered.

"Danny . . . ?" my mother said.

"Why are you out here?" I asked. "It's a bit – windy, isn't it?"

She wrapped her jacket tighter around her. "It sure is. But I was just thinking . . . after Julia called and told me about you finding the money Arvie had buried . . . I was just wondering."

"Wondering what?"

"Do you think your father might have buried something back here? The way Uncle Arvie buried something in *his* garden?"

"I don't know."

"Oh well, it's probably a silly idea," she said. "Let's go inside. I have some good news for you."

CHAPTER FOURTEEN
A Wish

"It's really Aunt Julia who has the good news," my mother said.

I felt terrible. All I could think about was Uncle Arvie, who had disappeared on the wind.

The phone rang. "Go on," my mother said. "Answer it. I bet it's Aunt Julia."

Reluctantly, I lifted the receiver.

"Danny? Is that you?" Aunt Julia said. "Did you happen to see a box of chocolates on the porch when you were here? Colin just phoned and said he left a box of chocolates."

"Well, I—"

"I'm not suggesting that *you* took them!" Aunt Julia said. "Anyone could have taken them. It was silly of him to leave them there in the first place."

"Yes, well—"

"I'm beginning to think he's rather a silly man. All that business with the wasps. *I* never saw any wasps, did you?" she asked.

"No, I—"

"Exactly. I think Colin is imagining things. He's a foolish man. Not nearly as interesting as your Uncle Arvie was. Colin is sort of a—a—"

"Sort of a beany booger?" I said.

"You sound just like Arvie," Aunt Julia said. "Thank you for reminding me of him. And thank you for finding Arvie's letter, and then for finding that beautiful painting of our honeymoon . . ." She sniffled. "And of course for finding the box today with all my letters and the money. I don't know how to thank you—"

"Oh, that's OK," I said. "It was fun finding those things."

"I think you deserve a reward," she said. "Anything you want. Anything at all. It's yours. What would you like?"

I thought. There were three things I wanted, but I knew that Aunt Julia could not give me two of those things. So I asked for the third.

I said, "In your garage is an old bike. Was that Uncle Arvie's?"

"That old thing?" Aunt Julia said. "That old rusty thing? Sure, it was Arvie's, but—"

"I have a little money saved to fix it up, but I

don't have enough. Maybe you could help me get it fixed . . . ?"

Aunt Julia said, "Of course I could. We'll get new tyres and have it painted and – are you sure that's what you want? You could have a whole new bicycle if you'd rather."

I thought about that. I was tempted to say, "Yes! A new bike!" but I didn't. Everything at Uncle Arvie's house was filled with mystery. "I'd rather have the one in the garage. Maybe some of Uncle Arvie will be in it – something magical and mysterious."

"Magical? Mysterious?" Julia said. "Arvie wasn't very magical or mysterious!"

"To me he was," I said. "In a – ghostly sort of way."

That night, in bed, I listened to the wind rattle against the cardboard taped to my window. I knew that Billy Baker would not be throwing any more rocks against these windows. I wondered if Billy was glad to know that ghosts existed. Maybe he could see ghosts because he needed a ghost.

Across the room was my empty desk. I wished Uncle Arvie were lying across it, with

his red hat poking off one end and his legs sticking straight out the other end. That was one of the things I wanted that Aunt Julia could not give me.

Uncle Arvie was probably far, far away now, sailing along on the wind, going wherever it took him. I found one bright star and made my wish. I wished for the other thing that Aunt Julia couldn't give me.

"Maybe this wind will bring more ghosts," I said. "Maybe this wind will bring me and Billy our *pepperonis*."

It *could*, I thought. This wind *could* bring our fathers sailing right through the window. You never know about ghosts.

A selected list of SHOCK SHOP titles available from
Macmillan Children's Books

The prices shown below are correct at the time of going to press.
However, Macmillan Publishers reserves the right to show new retail
prices on covers which may differ from those previously advertised.

K. M. Peyton *Stealaway*	0 330 39739 7	£3.99
Jenny Nimmo *The Bodigulpa*	0 330 39750 8	£3.99
Vivian French *Wicked Chickens*	0 330 41575 1	£3.99
Jan Mark *Long Lost*	0 330 39749 4	£3.99
Terence Blacker *You Have Ghost-Mail*	0 330 39699 4	£3.99
Jeanne Willis *The Beast of Crowsfoot Cottage*	0 330 41569 7	£3.99
Adèle Geras *Goodbye Tommy Blue*	0 330 41570 0	£3.99
Susan Price *Olly Spellmaker and the Hairy Horror* *Olly Spellmaker and the Sulky Smudge*	0 330 42119 0 0 330 41582 4	£3.99 £3.99
Dino Anatasio and Jane O'Connor *Watch Out!*	0 330 43415 2	£3.99
J. Burchett and S. Vogler *Phantom Fun!*	0 330 43416 0	£4.99

All Pan Macmillan titles can be ordered from our website,
www.panmacmillan.com, or from your local bookshop and
are also available by post from:

Bookpost, PO Box 29, Douglas, Isle of Man IM99 1BQ
Credit cards accepted. For details:
Telephone: 01624 677237
Fax: 01624 670923
E-mail: bookshop@enterprise.net
www.bookpost.co.uk

Free postage and packing in the United Kingdom